To Emily,

Sally K Ride

10/18/95

SALLY RIDE & TAM O'SHAUGHNESSY

THE THIRD PLANET

EXPLORING THE EARTH FROM SPACE

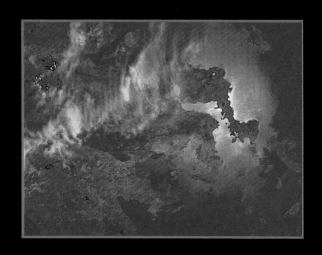

CROWN PUBLISHERS, INC.

NEW YORK

▶ *Florida, through a window of the Space Shuttle.*

Previous page: Greece and the Aegean Sea.

Photograph on page 7 © James Martin; page 33 courtesy
Robert M. Carey, NOAA Satellite Research Laboratory;
page 46 © Scientific American Inc., George V. Kelvin. All
other photographs courtesy of National Aeronautics and
Space Administration (NASA).

Published by Crown Publishers Inc., a Random House
company, 201 East 50th Street, New York, New York 10022

CROWN is a trademark of Crown Publishers, Inc.

Manufactured in United States of America

Library of Congress Cataloging-in-Publication Data

Ride, Sally.
The third planet: exploring the earth from space / Sally
Ride, Tam O'Shaughnessy.
                              p. cm.
Includes index.
Summary: Astronaut Sally Ride examines how the earth is
studied from space, its critical relationship with the other
planets in the solar system, and some of earth's features,
including climate, orbits, atmosphere, and light.
1. Earth—Juvenile literature. 2. Astronautics in
astronomy—Juvenile literature. [1. Earth. 2. Astronomy.
3. Astronautics.] I. O'Shaughnessy, Tam. II. Title.
QB631.4.R53   1994
525—dc20   '92-40609

ISBN 0-517-59361-0 (trade)
       0-517-59362-9 (lib. bdg.)

10 9 8 7 6 5 4 3 2

TO OUR MOTHERS,

WHO SHOWED US HOW TO EXPLORE

WHEN WE WERE YOUNG

THROUGH THE SMALL WINDOWS OF THE SPACE SHUTTLE, I looked down on Earth and saw the oceans and land that make up our planet. The view was spectacular.

Circling 200 miles above the Earth, I saw the atmosphere—just a thin, blue band above the horizon—separating Earth from the blackness of space. I watched a huge hurricane swirling in the Atlantic Ocean, and an enormous dust storm blowing across the entire Sahara Desert. Some nights, I saw lightning light up the clouds below, and jump from cloud to cloud across the sky. One night, as the Shuttle passed over Florida, I watched all the cities from Miami to New York twinkle in the darkness.

The Space Shuttle streaks through space at 17,500 miles per hour. It crosses the United States in just a few minutes, and circles the whole planet in just an hour and a half. Floating at a Space Shuttle window, I could take pictures of giant glaciers in Alaska one minute and of the shallow waters off the Florida coast 15 minutes later. By the time I returned to Earth, I had seen most of the planet. I understood how much we could learn by studying Earth from above.

Many satellites have the same view that I had. As they orbit the Earth, they gather information that helps us put together a picture of our complicated planet. This book is about exploring the Earth from space.

Greece and the Mediterranean Sea (left) and a snow-filled volcanic crater in Alaska (above)—both photos taken during my second flight on board the Space Shuttle.

ORBITS

Like the Space Shuttle, Earth-observing satellites travel in orbit around the Earth. A satellite is lifted into orbit by a rocket, or by the Space Shuttle and its rockets. A rocket has to lift the satellite above the atmosphere, then get it moving fast enough in the right direction for it to stay in orbit after the rocket burns out.

A satellite is held in orbit by the pull of Earth's gravity. Gravity makes the satellite continuously fall toward Earth. As it is falling, though, the satellite is traveling so fast toward the horizon that it always misses hitting the Earth and instead "falls around" the planet.

Like the Shuttle, most Earth-observing satellites are in orbit a few hundred miles above the Earth. A satellite goes around and around the planet, retracing its path in space. While it is repeating the same path, the Earth rotates underneath it. This means that the satellite passes over different parts of the planet on each orbit. The Earth makes one complete turn every 24 hours. During this time, a satellite can see a lot of the planet.

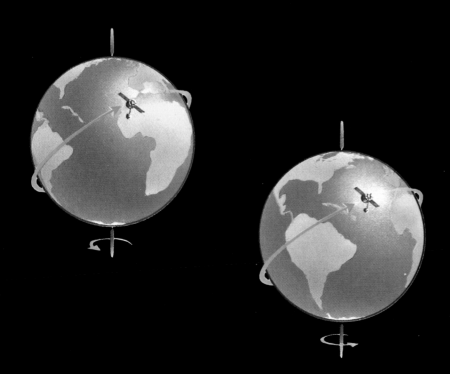

Because of the Earth's rotation, a satellite will pass over a different part of the planet on each orbit.

Mars

Earth

SUN

MERCURY

VENUS

EARTH

MARS

JUPITER

SATURN

URANUS

NEPTUNE

PLUTO

Venus

*The Solar System.
(Sizes and distances
are not shown to scale.)*

ᴇᴀʀᴛʜ, ᴛʜᴇ ᴛʜɪʀᴅ ᴘʟᴀɴᴇᴛ ꜰʀᴏᴍ ᴛʜᴇ ꜱᴜɴ, is different from the other planets in our solar system. It is the only planet that has liquid water. Because there is water, life can exist.

Mars and Venus, Earth's nearest neighbors, are similar in size and composition, but they are very different from Earth. Venus is too hot for liquid water to exist. Radar images from the *Magellan* spacecraft show a hot, dry planet with high plateaus, long valleys, and rugged mountains. But green plants and blue waters are missing from the landscape.

Long ago water probably flowed on Mars, but today Mars is too cold. Now the water is frozen in the ground and in polar icecaps. If water once existed, perhaps primitive life did too. The *Viking* spacecraft analyzed samples of soil but found no evidence of life. *Viking* sent back pictures of a red, rocky planet that is cold, dry, and lifeless.

Earth is special because of its distance from the sun. Earth receives less of the sun's warmth than Venus, but more than Mars. Our planet is just the right temperature for water to exist as a liquid. If Earth were much colder, all the water would be frozen; if it were much warmer, all the water would evaporate.

Earth is an oasis in our otherwise lifeless solar system

More than 70 percent of the Earth's surface is covered with water. Nearly all of that water is in the deep, blue, saltwater oceans. The oceans fill huge basins in the Earth's crust, and are home to much of the plant and animal life on the planet.

The rest of the Earth's surface is land. Like Mars and Venus, Earth has mountains, valleys, and deserts. But mountains on Earth are covered with green forests, the valleys may have rivers running through them, and even the deserts are alive with plants and animals.

Earth is surrounded by a thin blanket of air called the atmosphere. The atmosphere is Earth's space suit. It is the air we breathe and our planet's shield against harmful ultraviolet light from the sun.

LIGHT

Red light, blue light, and the rest of the colors we can see are known as <u>visible light</u>. One way to picture light is as a wave traveling through space. The wave carries energy and travels at a rate of 186,000 miles per second—the "speed of light."

If you move your hand up and down in a bathtub full of water, waves (in this case, water waves) will travel across the tub. The distance between the wave crests is called the <u>wavelength</u>.

WAVELENGTH

If you move your hand slowly, the wave crests are far apart, and the wavelength is long; if you move your hand more rapidly, they are closer together, and the wavelength is shorter. The difference between the colors that make up visible light is just a difference in wavelength: red light has the longest wavelength and violet light has the shortest.

But there are some forms of light that are invisible to our eyes, such as infrared light (which has wavelengths longer than red) and ultraviolet light (which has wavelengths shorter than violet)

The parts of the planet—the oceans, atmosphere, land, and living things—are connected. Winds in the atmosphere drive ocean currents; green plants add oxygen to the air and remove carbon dioxide from it; volcanoes throw tons of gas and dust into the atmosphere from deep inside the Earth.

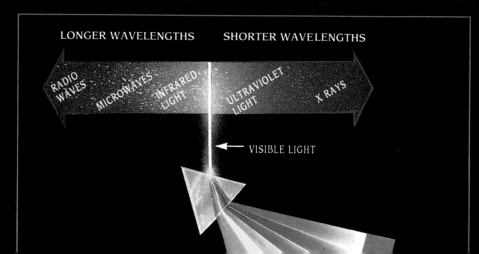

LONGER WAVELENGTHS   SHORTER WAVELENGTHS

RADIO WAVES   MICROWAVES   INFRARED LIGHT   ULTRAVIOLET LIGHT   X RAYS

← VISIBLE LIGHT

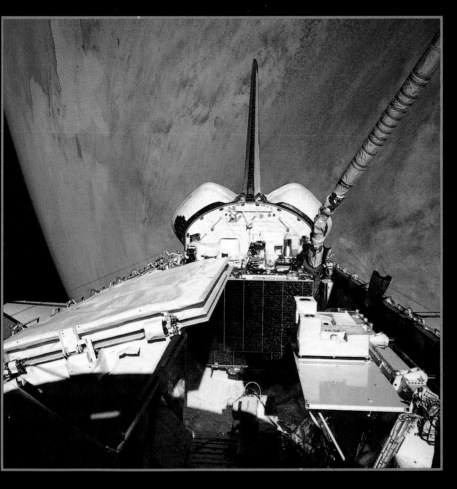

A satellite is lifted from the payload bay of the Space Shuttle.

Astronauts take pictures of the Earth with ordinary cameras. These cameras detect visible light—they record what a scene looks like to the human eye. But cameras cannot record everything. A camera can't take pictures at night; it can't see through clouds; it can't determine what the atmosphere is made of.

Other instruments "see" other types of electromagnetic radiation. For example, some detectors measure infrared light that the rocks, soil, plants, and water emit after they have been warmed by sunlight. Since infrared light is emitted by an object in the night as well as in the daytime, these detectors can "see in the dark."

Gases in the atmosphere also emit infrared light. By recording this light, satellite instruments can determine what the atmosphere is made of, its temperature, and the speed of the winds.

Radars in space send out pulses of microwaves that travel down to the Earth, then are reflected back toward space and received by the radar's antenna. Different surfaces reflect the pulses differently, so returning pulses carry information about the ground where they hit. Radars are used to study everything from ice sheets to ocean currents. Because some radars emit pulses that pass through clouds, they can study the Earth even through overcast skies.

Looking at the Earth from space, scientists can study connections like these on a global scale. Satellite instruments can watch an ocean current move heat from the equator to the poles, monitor the effects of air pollution on the health of a forest, and observe the effect of a large volcano on the world's climate.

Scientists use many types of instruments to look down at the Earth. All of them measure light in one form or another. Some instruments can "see" infrared light that our eyes cannot; others analyze visible light in different ways. Many of these instruments can see in the dark. Some can also see through clouds. Together they collect information that helps us understand our planet: its atmosphere, its oceans, its land, its life, and the connections between them.

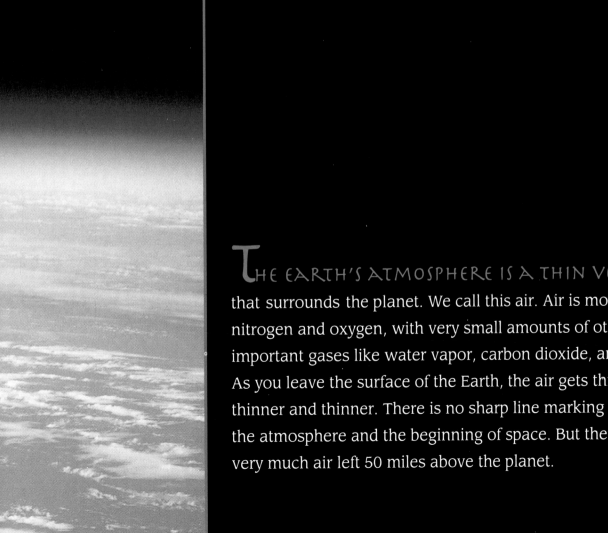

THE EARTH'S ATMOSPHERE IS A THIN VEIL of gas
that surrounds the planet. We call this air. Air is mostly
nitrogen and oxygen, with very small amounts of other
important gases like water vapor, carbon dioxide, and ozone.
As you leave the surface of the Earth, the air gets thinner and
thinner and thinner. There is no sharp line marking the end of
the atmosphere and the beginning of space. But there is not
very much air left 50 miles above the planet.

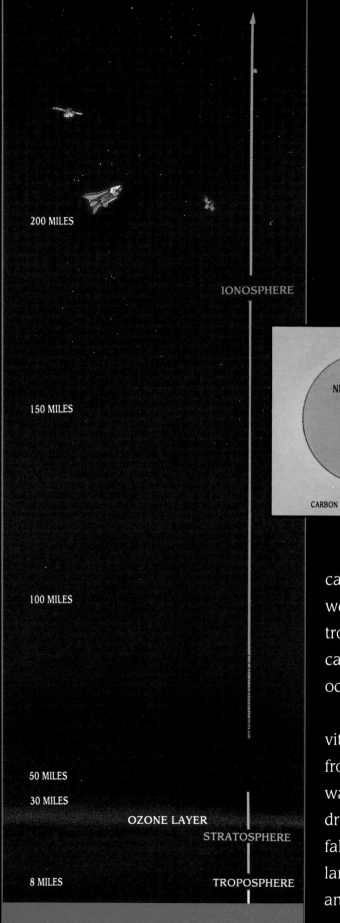

200 MILES

IONOSPHERE

150 MILES

100 MILES

50 MILES

30 MILES

OZONE LAYER

STRATOSPHERE

8 MILES

TROPOSPHERE

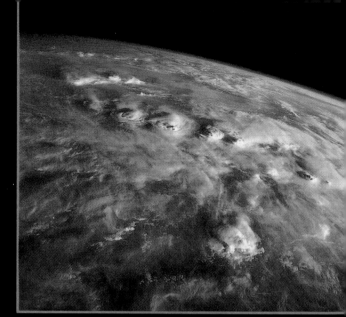

▲ *Thunderstorms in the troposphere.*

◀ *This chart shows the proportions of different gases in the Earth's atmosphere.*

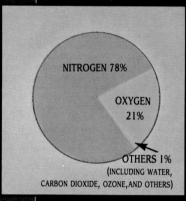

NITROGEN 78%

OXYGEN 21%

OTHERS 1%
(INCLUDING WATER, CARBON DIOXIDE, OZONE, AND OTHERS)

The part of the atmosphere closest to Earth is called the *troposphere*. Most of the Earth's weather is in this layer of air. Winds in the troposphere move heat around the planet; they carry water in the form of clouds from the oceans to the land.

The movement of water around the world is vital to life on Earth. The sun evaporates water from the oceans. Once in the atmosphere, the water rises, then condenses into very small droplets that form clouds. This water eventually falls back to Earth as rain. If the rain falls over land, it wets the soil, collects in lakes and rivers, and is available to the plants and animals that need it to survive.

Hurricanes form in the tropics over large areas of warm water. They gather strength by drawing energy and moisture from the ocean. Once a storm's winds grow to more than 74 miles per hour, it is called a hurricane.

These are pictures of Hurricane Kamysi, a huge storm in the Indian Ocean. Strong winds

OZONE AND "CFCs"

Sometimes a chemical that appears beneficial can cause unexpected problems.

In the late 1920s, scientists created a very useful group of chemicals called chlorofluorocarbons—or "CFCs." They seemed like the perfect chemicals because they are not toxic and they last a very long time. Since then, CFCs have found many important uses, including as coolants in refrigerators, freezers, and air conditioners.

Almost 50 years later, scientists discovered that these chemicals were slowly destroying the ozone layer in the Earth's atmosphere.

CFCs last long enough that they eventually rise all the way up into the stratosphere. Once they are up that high, ultraviolet light from the sun breaks them apart, releasing chlorine. The chlorine reacts with ozone and destroys it.

The nations of the world have realized that the thinning of the ozone layer is a serious problem, and have agreed to limit the use of CFCs. Chemists are now trying to find other chemicals to use instead of CFCs.

The huge thunderclouds in the picture below reach to the top of the troposphere. But the atmosphere doesn't end there. The air above the troposphere is called the *stratosphere*. The air in the stratosphere is very thin—too thin to breathe and too thin for most airplanes to fly.

The Earth's ozone layer is in the stratosphere. Although there is very little ozone, it is very important to life on Earth because it absorbs some of the sun's ultraviolet light. Without ozone, too much ultraviolet light would reach the surface of the Earth and damage living cells.

Scientists are keenly interested in the ozone layer. There is evidence that the ozone is slowly being destroyed by certain human-made chemicals that drift up into the stratosphere. It is difficult to study this part of the atmosphere from the surface of the Earth because the lower atmosphere gets in the way, but instruments in space can study it from above.

The astronaut who photographed this sunset was looking toward the Earth's horizon. Most instruments that study the stratosphere also point toward the horizon. They observe infrared light given off by gases at different heights, and gather valuable information on the ozone layer and the chemicals that affect it.

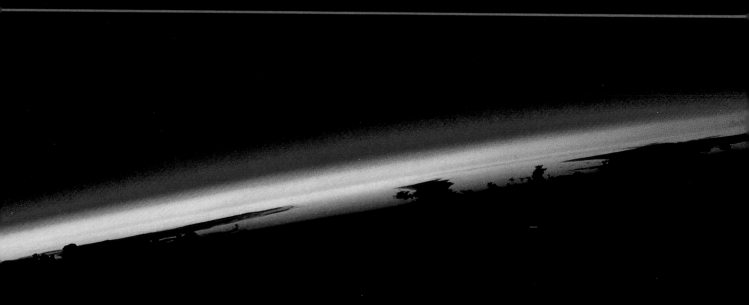

The Earth's atmosphere does not end abruptly. Even above the stratosphere, there are a few oxygen and nitrogen atoms. A glowing aurora like the one above occurs when high-energy particles that stream out of the sun collide with these atoms. The collisions cause the atoms to emit light. The green light is given off by oxygen atoms, the traces of red (*top right*) by nitrogen and oxygen. The result is spectacular.

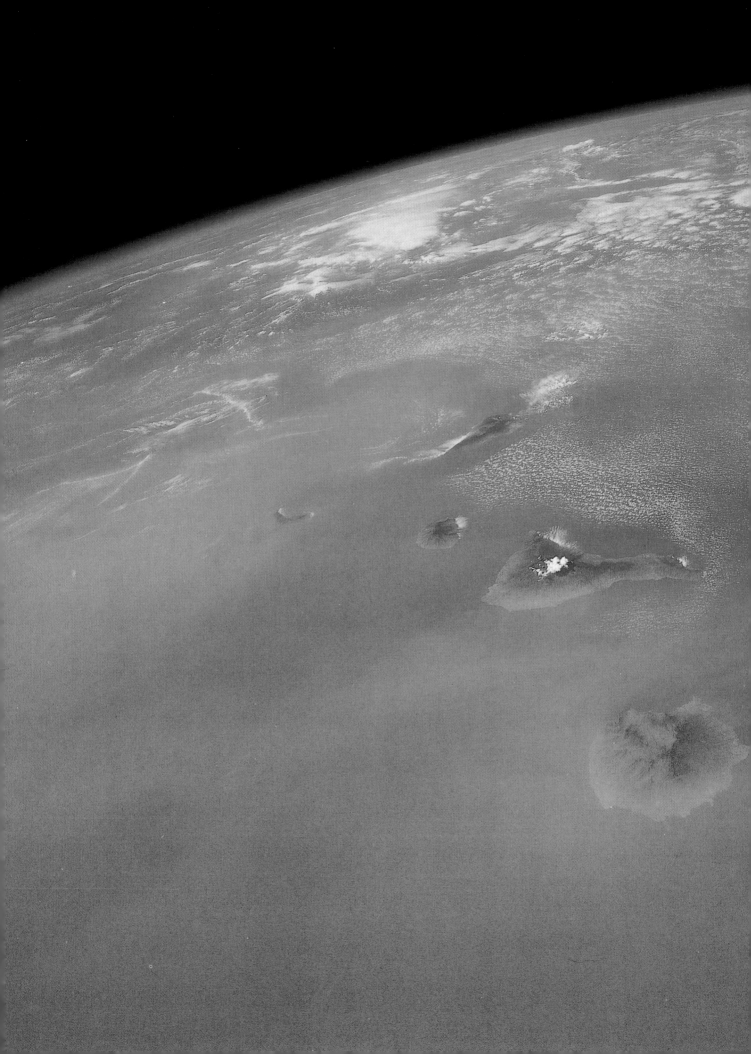

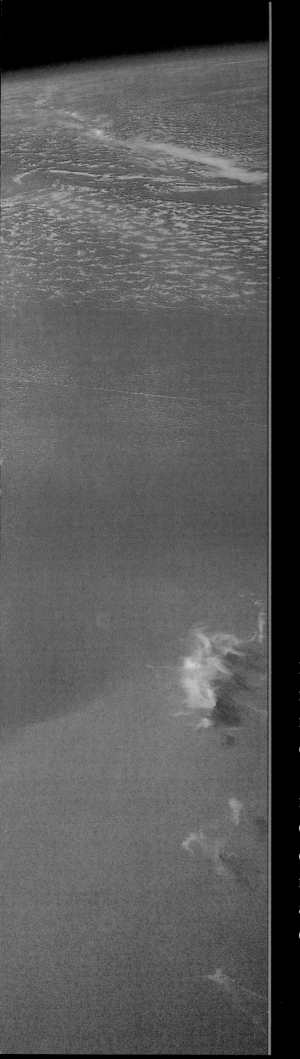

Oceans cover much of the earth.

Because the oceans are so large, the best way to study many of their features is from space. It takes a ship many days to cross the Atlantic Ocean. A spacecraft can cover the same distance in only a few minutes.

The depth of the oceans varies dramatically. The sea floor has trenches that are deeper than the Grand Canyon—and thousands of volcanic mountains that climb toward the ocean surface. Some of these mountains reach high enough to peek above the water and form islands, like the Canary Islands in the Atlantic Ocean (*left*).

In this photograph of the Bahama Islands, areas of lighter blue show where the water is shallow. These areas drop off steeply into deep ocean (dark blue).

The oceans are not calm, smooth, motionless pools of water. The water rises and falls with the daily tides. Winds in the atmosphere kick up waves. Currents that act like long conveyor belts move rivers of salt water around the world.

Winds drive currents near the surface of the ocean. The Gulf Stream is a major current that flows up the east coast of the United States. It helps move heat around the planet, carrying warm water from the tropics into the colder North Atlantic Ocean. As it travels north, it loses some of its heat to the atmosphere and some to the cooler water. Without currents like the Gulf Stream, the tropics would be much hotter than they are, and the poles would be much colder.

The image below of the North Atlantic Ocean was made from data collected by an infrared instrument that measures temperature. The Gulf Stream stands out clearly because it is so much warmer than the surrounding ocean. The image has been artificially colored, with each color representing a different temperature. The coldest water is shown in dark blue. Light blue, green, yellow, and orange are warmer; the warmest waters are red and brown. With this color scheme, the warm Gulf Stream looks like a tongue of red flowing into the cooler North Atlantic Ocean. This current carries more water than all the rivers in the world.

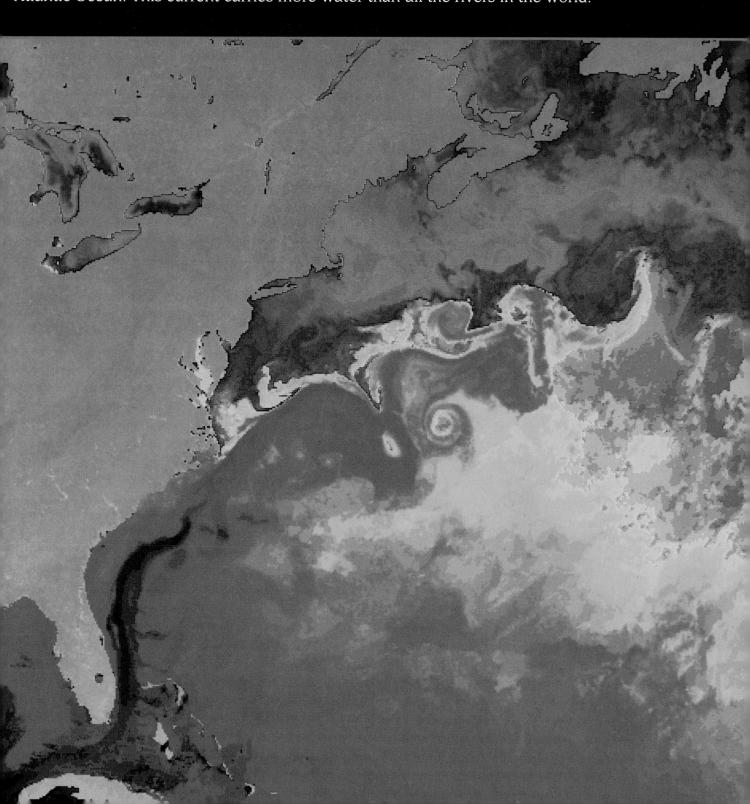

Microscopic ocean plants, called *phytoplankton*, are critical to life in the ocean. They reproduce in huge numbers when nutrients from the bottom of the ocean are brought up to the surface by deep ocean currents. When there are enough of them, they can even be seen from space. In the photograph below, billions of phytoplankton add a green color to the water off the coast of Namibia.

Phytoplankton live near the surface, where they use the energy of sunlight to turn carbon dioxide and water into food. Only plants can do this. The process is called *photosynthesis*.

The entire ocean food chain depends on phytoplankton. Microscopic animals, called *zooplankton*, eat the phytoplankton, small fish eat the zooplankton, larger fish eat the small fish, and animals like seals and pelicans eat the larger fish.

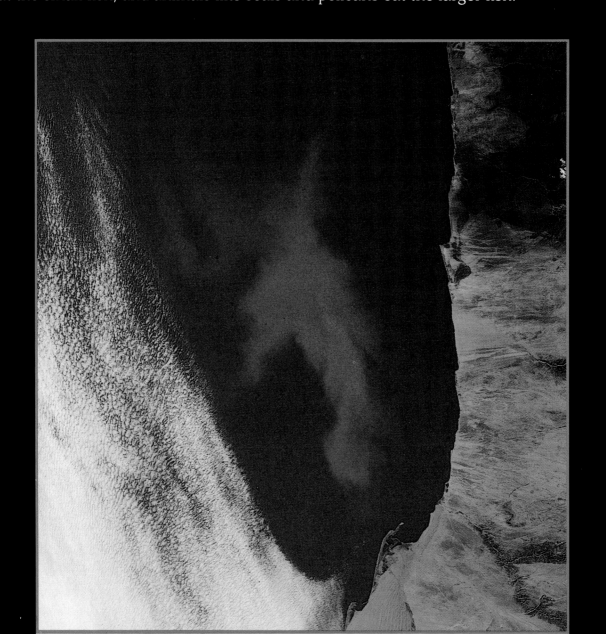

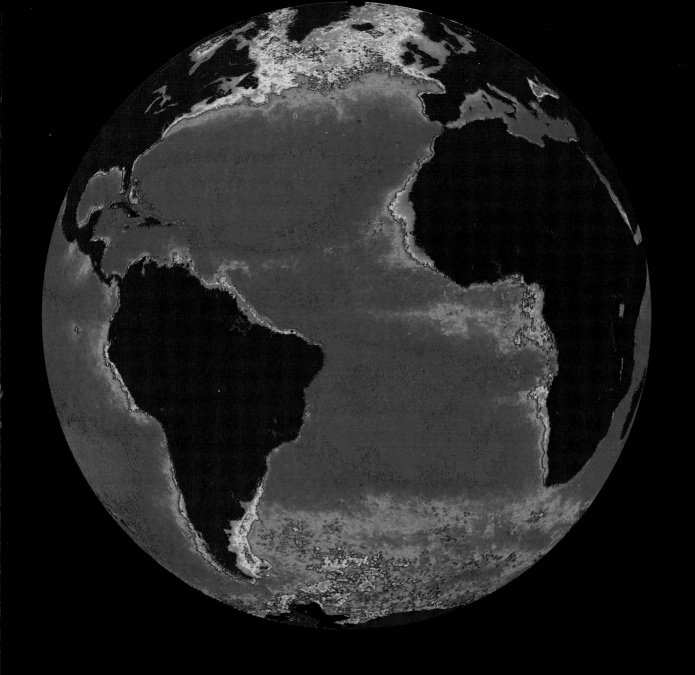

The location of phytoplankton is important because where there are phytoplankton, there are other ocean animals. Instruments in space can look for green color in the water and map the phytoplankton in the world's oceans. This picture was put together from data collected over a period of 32 months. Purples and blues are areas of no phytoplankton; red areas have the most. The picture shows that some parts of the ocean are barren, while others are exploding with life.

Almost all of the water on Earth is in the saltwater oceans. The rest is fresh water. Some of this fresh water is in rivers and lakes, but most of it is locked up in ice.

The amount of ice on Earth depends on the planet's climate. Through the ages, the Earth has experienced many long periods of cooling, called ice ages, followed by long periods of warming. During ice ages, snow and ice accumulate, and giant glaciers spread over much of the planet. When the climate warms again, the ice slowly melts and the glaciers shrink.

For the past 10,000 years the Earth has been in a warm period. Even so, there is still a huge amount of ice on the planet. The continent of Antarctica lies buried under an icecap two miles thick; the sea around the North Pole is mostly under ice, even in the summer; glaciers still flow, like giant ice rivers, from ice fields in many parts of the world.

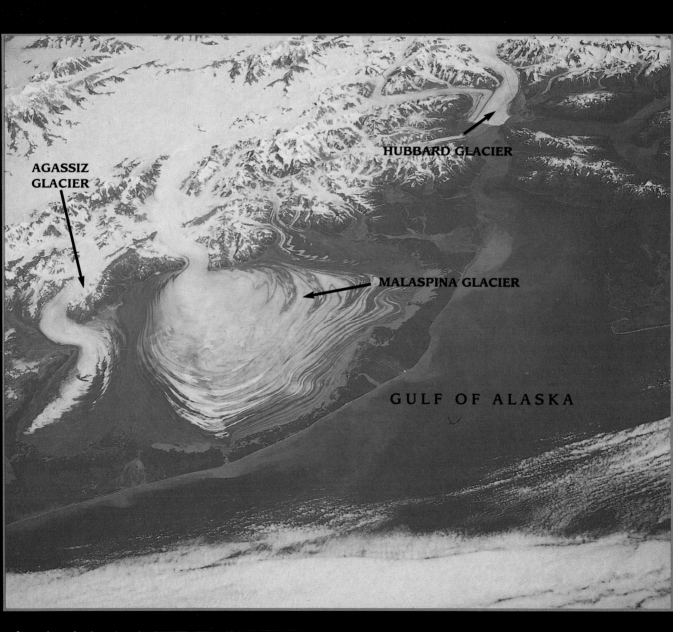

Three ice glaciers in Alaska. Ice from the Malaspina Glacier forms a distinctive ring pattern as it surges toward the ocean.

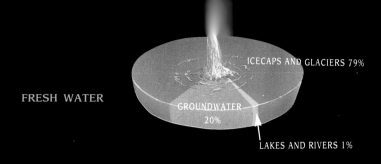

FRESH WATER

ICECAPS AND GLACIERS 79%

GROUNDWATER 20%

LAKES AND RIVERS 1%

The chart above shows the proportions of salt water and fresh water on Earth. The chart below shows the different forms in which fresh water is found: frozen in icecaps and glaciers; flowing in lakes and rivers; and as ground water (underground water that supplies springs and wells).

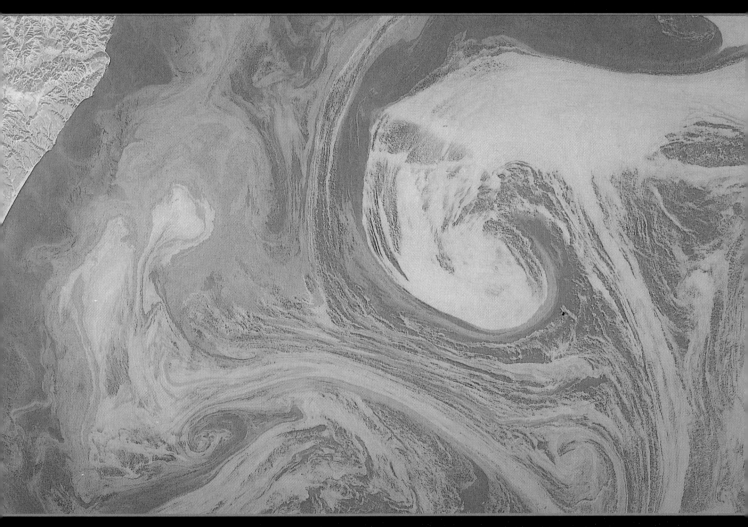

Swirls of sea ice off the coast of the Kamchatka peninsula in northeastern Russia.

Some scientists think that the Earth's climate is slowly warming. Accurate measurements of the ice near the poles may provide evidence one way or the other. Satellite radars can measure the size of the ice sheets quite accurately because radar pulses are reflected differently by ice than by water or land. Measurements taken over several years will show whether the ice sheets are slowly growing or shrinking, and will

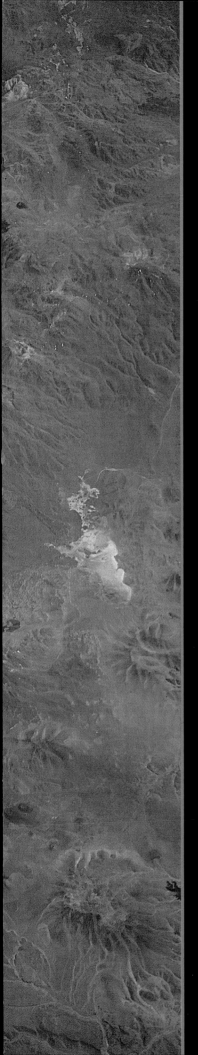

The Andes mountain range in South America.

It is hard to imagine the land changing, but it does. The face of our planet is continually being reshaped and resurfaced by forces deep inside the Earth. Over millions and millions of years these forces move entire continents, recycle rocks and land, and build enormous mountain ranges.

Only a few decades ago, scientists believed that the Earth's crust did not move. Now we know that it is broken into distinct pieces, called *plates*. These plates float on the hot, sometimes molten, rock found 20 to 50 miles beneath the surface. They actually move across the face of the Earth. The plates move very, very slowly—only a few inches each year. But over millions of years they can travel a long way.

In some places, plates grind past each other; in other places, they collide head-on. Fifty million years ago, the Himalayan mountains (*below*) did not exist. They were formed when the plate carrying India crashed headlong into Asia. The land where the two continents met began to crumple, and the world's largest mountain range was formed. The Himalayas now separate the high plateau of Tibet from the low plains of India. The plate carrying India is still moving north, at a rate of nearly two inches each year. The Himalayas are still being pushed up, growing about a tenth of an inch per year.

SEA OF
GALILEE

DEAD
SEA

The long, straight line in this picture of the Middle East is a rift that is opening up as a result of the very slow movement of Israel away from Jordan. The rift runs from the Sea of Galilee south to the Dead Sea and beyond. Millions of years from now the rift will have opened, and the two sides will be separated by a sea.

How can space observations help our understanding of things that happen so slowly? Although it may seem hard to believe, it is possible to use satellites to measure the motions of the Earth's crust. Scientists on Earth bounce laser light off mirror-covered satellites and measure the time it takes for the light to return. From this they can determine the laser's location very precisely. Doing this over and over allows scientists to measure motions as tiny as a tenth of an inch per year, and to watch the plates move from year to year.

The slow movements of the Earth's plates sometimes have sudden and dramatic consequences. In some places, two plates come together and one is pushed under the other, back into the hot interior of the Earth. Some of it melts, forming molten rock, called *magma,* which may erupt to the surface. The result is a volcano. When large volcanoes erupt, they throw material from deep inside the Earth high into the atmosphere.

The huge crater on Sumbawa Island in Indonesia (*above*) was created by one of the largest volcanic eruptions in history. In 1815, the Tambora volcano erupted with so much force that it left this crater, almost four miles across, and rocketed gas and dust all the way up into the stratosphere. This material quickly spread around the world. It formed a thin veil that blocked out some of the sun's light, and affected the climate all around the planet. In the northeastern United States, the year after the Tambora eruption became known as "the year without a summer"; it was so cold that there were snowstorms in June.

An eruption as large as Tambora is very unusual. But smaller, less destructive volcanoes occur often. An astronaut circling the Earth in the Space Shuttle can expect to see a volcano erupting every few days. Many are in remote areas of the world and would not be reported if they weren't seen from space.

One of the largest volcanoes of this century erupted while satellites were watching. These globes were made by computers using data collected before and after the eruption of Mount Pinatubo in the Philippines in 1991. They show that gas and dust from the volcano circled the Earth. Scientists estimate that the average temperature of the planet dropped about one degree Fahrenheit in the months following this huge eruption.

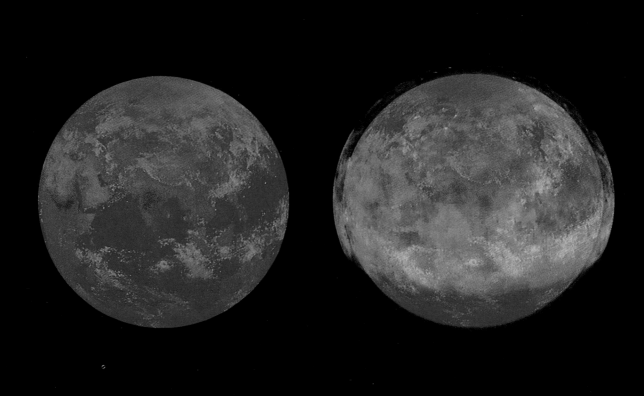

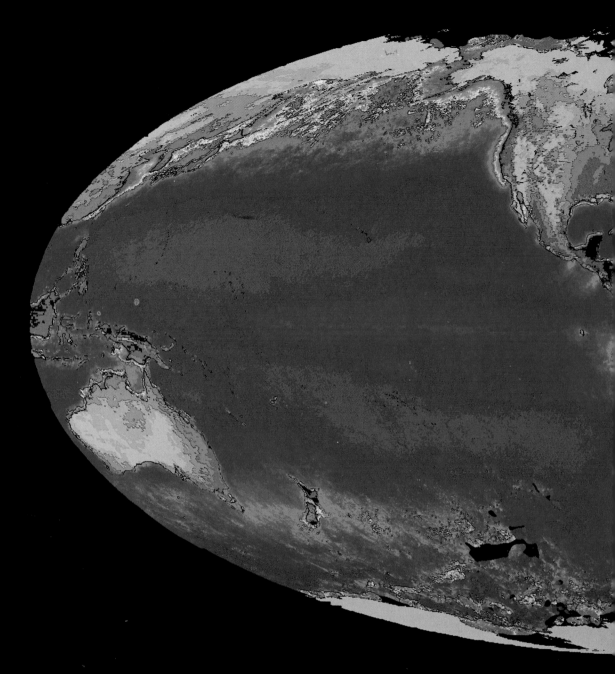

THE LIVING THINGS OF THE EARTH INHABIT a thin
realm of water, air, and land called the *biosphere*. The biosphere
extends several miles up into the atmosphere and several feet
down into the soil. It includes rivers and lakes and reaches deep
into the oceans.

This image, put together from satellite data, is the first global
map of plant life in the biosphere. It shows the location of
phytoplankton in the water and plants on land. Because there
are other living creatures wherever there are plants, the map
shows the distribution of life on Earth.

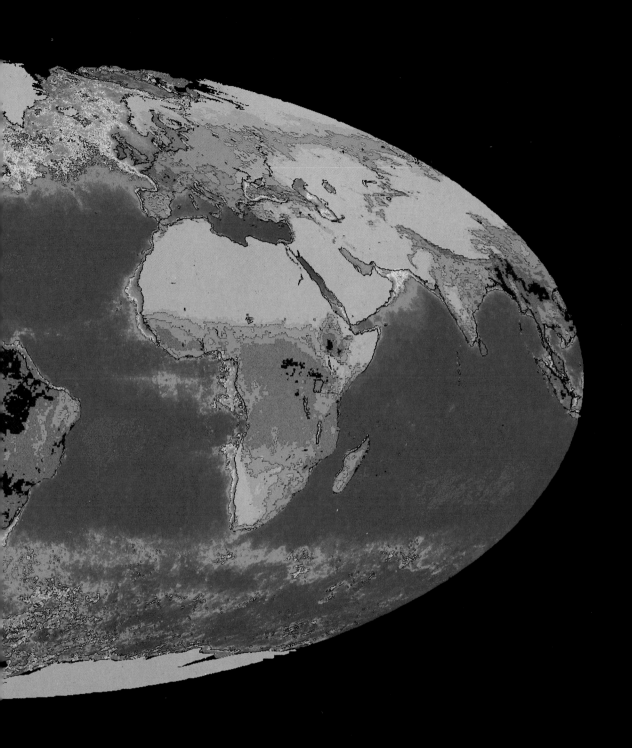

On land, some areas are rich in plant life (green), while others are too hot or cold or dry for plants to flourish (yellow). In the ocean, the richest areas of phytoplankton are along the coasts (yellow, orange, and red), where rivers and deep ocean currents bring nutrients to the waters. The deserts, the north and south poles, and vast areas of ocean are almost barren, while forests and coastal waters are teeming with life.

Deserts like the Sahara in Africa, the Gobi in Asia, and the Great Sandy Desert in Australia are dry, desolate places where water is extremely rare and precious. It seldom rains, but when it does, small lakes and ponds suddenly appear. Millions of seeds, waiting in the dry ground, soak up tiny drops of water and sprout to life. Desert animals drink and bathe in the water, which will soon disappear. Because the rain never lasts long, the only plants and animals that live in the desert are those that are able to conserve water. But some years there is so little rain that even the plants and animals of the desert go thirsty.

Satellite data show that during years of drought the Sahara Desert spreads south into the grasslands of the Sahel (1984, below). The computer picture from 1988 shows that when the rains return, a wave of vegetation reappears across the grasslands.

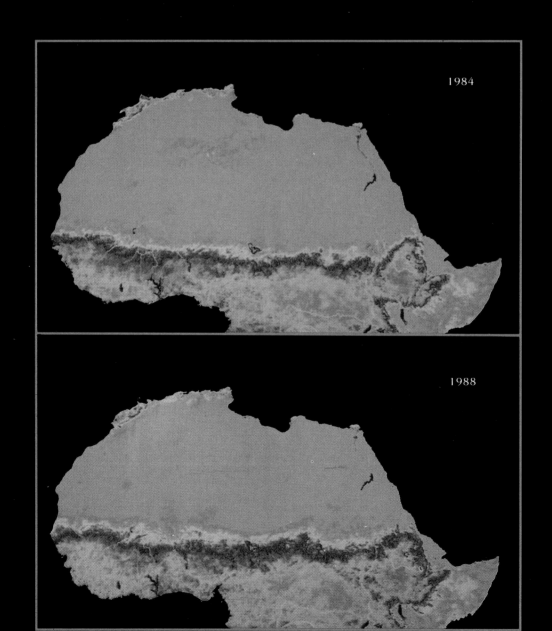

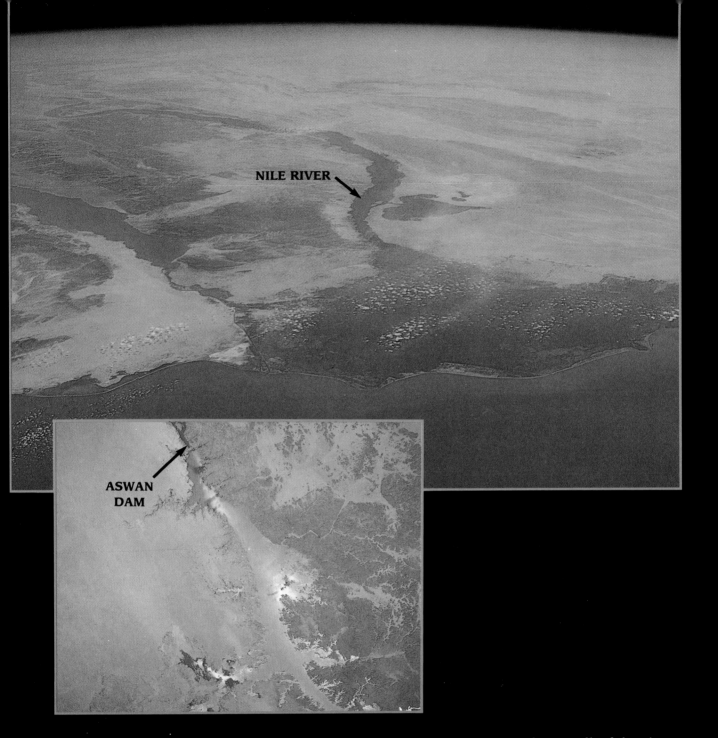

NILE RIVER

ASWAN
DAM

Not many people live in the desert. Those who do live near water. Almost all of the 60 million people in Egypt live along the Nile River. They depend on the Nile for many things, including irrigation of the land along its banks. The agricultural land hugging the Nile (*top*) looks like a green ribbon winding through the dry Sahara Desert.

Lake Nasser is a human-made lake farther up the river. It was created when the Aswan Dam was built across the Nile. The smaller picture was taken after several years of drought, when the water in the lake was very low. The white outline around the edges of the lake and the gray lake bed in the lower left are under water when the lake is full. Satellite instruments measure the size of this lake and others in deserts, to help people manage their water.

In some places near the equator, rain falls year-round. The warm temperatures and wet weather result in lush tropical rain forests in Central and South America, Africa, and Asia. The rain forests are alive with thousands of kinds of plants and animals. Colorful birds whistle and squawk, strange insects click and buzz, and bright-eyed monkeys scream as they swing through the jungle. Giant trees, wrapped in thick vines, shade the ferns and mosses that cover the wet forest floor.

There are more species of animals and plants in the rain forests than anywhere else on Earth—so many that most have not even been named. People living in the forests and, more recently, scientists have learned that many of the exotic plants are valuable. Some of them are sources of food, and others are sources of important medicines.

In some parts of the world, the rain forests are in danger. Large sections of the Amazon rain forest in Brazil are being cut down and burned so that the land can be used for farming and cattle ranching. Until recently, the government of Brazil encouraged this because it gave people their own land and a way to make a living. But tropical soils are not good for growing crops or grazing cattle. After only a few years, the nutrients in the soil are completely used up; farmers and ranchers must move on, and clear new sections of the forest.

As the trees disappear, so do countless rare plants and animals that make their homes in the rain forest. The people of Brazil have begun to realize that a healthy rain forest is valuable and should be protected. Because satellite pictures show rain forest destruction very clearly, they are being used to monitor this huge jungle. Even a rain forest the size of the Amazon can be photographed in only a few hours by satellite.

This image of the border between Mexico and Guatemala shows thriving, uncut rain forest on the Guatemalan side (right). On the Mexican side (left) the land has been cleared to grow corn and graze cattle.

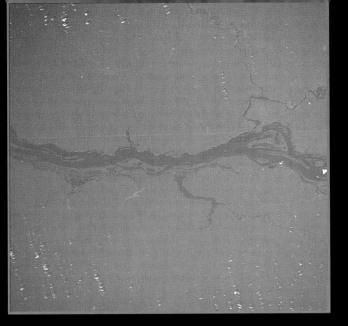
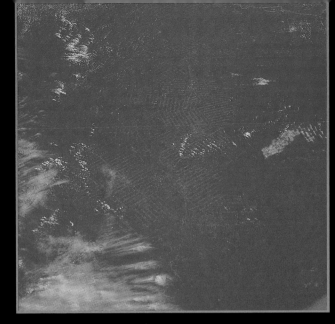

Above: Dense, undisturbed rain forest surrounding the Rio Negro river in the Amazon region (left) and smoke rising from fires as the forest is cleared (right). Below: This picture of part of Brazil shows roads cutting into the rain forest and patches of forest cleared away near these roads.

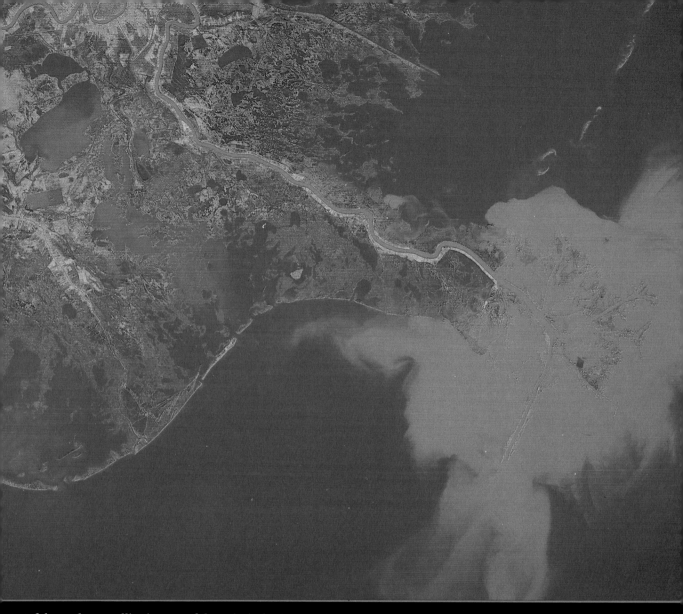

▲ *A false-color satellite image of the Mississippi River delta.*

Some of the richest ecosystems on the planet are found where large rivers empty into the ocean. These areas, where fresh water mixes with salt water, are called river *deltas*. From space, the Mississippi River delta looks like a giant bird's foot. The mighty river collects soil and nutrients as they drain off the land, and carries them to the sea. When the Mississippi River meets the Gulf of Mexico, it drops its load and new land is created. The mud flats, small islands, and salt marshes are packed with life. Flocks of birds feast on small worms; rows of turtles bask in the sun; frogs hide in the tall marsh grasses.

The Mississippi delta depends on the steady supply of soil and nutrients washed down by the river. Satellite instruments watch the muddy river dump its load and keep track of the

The Ganges River, which empties into the Indian Ocean on the border between India and Bangladesh, forms the largest delta in the world. It is a constantly changing maze of mud flats and marshes. Like the Mississippi delta, it relies on the soil and nutrients carried down by the river. Mangrove trees, which can survive in the shallow, salty water, are the heart of this ecosystem. Their tangled roots anchor the mud flats, creating a vast stretch of mangrove marshes.

The dark area in the picture below is a wildlife preserve in the Ganges delta called the Sundarbans. It is the largest mangrove forest in the world. Here, Bengal tigers roam the dense forest, and crocodiles keep watch in the swamps.

The land around the Sundarbans is home to one of the largest human populations on Earth. Once this part of the delta was also covered in thick mangrove forests. But now most of the trees have been cut down. The marshes have been drained to grow food for the huge population. Without the protection of the mangrove trees, the delta is being worn away by heavy rains and stormy seas.

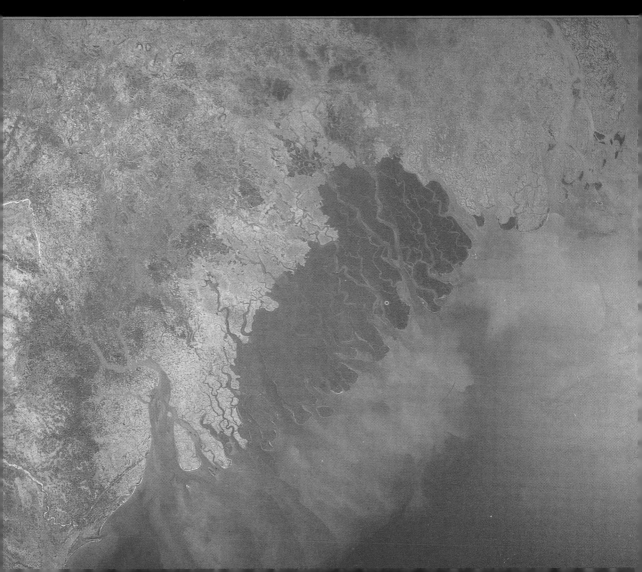

When the number of human beings on the planet was small, their effect on the planet was small. But over the past 100 years, the number of people on Earth has exploded. Now our presence is felt around the world—and our impact can be seen even from space.

Huge cities spread out over miles of land. Los Angeles (*above*) and its surrounding communities are home to more than 10 million people.

With more and more people on the planet, more and more land must be used to grow food. the Imperial Valley near Los Angeles, dry desert has been turned into fertile fields. The lake this picture holds salt water, not fresh water, and cannot be used for irrigation. Fresh water s to be pumped miles and miles across the desert to water the plants and make them oom.

IMPERIAL VALLEY

THE GREENHOUSE EFFECT

Most of the sun's energy comes to Earth in the form of visible light. Visible light passes freely through Earth's atmosphere and heats the surface of the planet. The warm Earth then radiates energy back toward space in the form of infrared light. But this infrared light does not pass freely through the atmosphere—some of it is trapped. This is called the <u>greenhouse effect</u> because the glass walls of a greenhouse also let visible light in but don't let infrared light out.

The Earth's atmosphere contains small amounts of water and carbon dioxide. These are called <u>greenhouse gases</u> because they are the ones that trap the infrared light, making the planet warmer than it would be if they were not there. In fact, without these gases, the Earth would be nearly 60 degrees Fahrenheit colder than it is!

Over the last 100 years, people have been adding lots of extra carbon dioxide to the atmosphere. Carbon dioxide is released when gasoline is burned in a car, when wood is burned in a fire, and when coal is burned in a power plant. As more carbon dioxide enters the air, more infrared light is trapped, and the Earth very slowly becomes warmer. Scientists predict that this will cause the average temperature of the planet to rise at least two degrees Fahrenheit in the next 50 years.

This sounds like a small change, but it would affect us all. Polar ice could melt, causing the level of the world's oceans to rise, and flooding some cities on the coast. Weather patterns around the planet could change: some desert lands could become very wet, and some farmlands could become desert.

Oil is our most important source of energy. It is used to heat homes and schools, and to make the gasoline that powers cars and airplanes.

Much of Earth's oil lies beneath the deserts of the Middle East. The picture above, taken in the early evening, shows the fires that burn natural gas off the tops of oil wells in the countries surrounding the Persian Gulf. The large bright patch in the center of the picture is the city of Riyadh in Saudi Arabia.

As the population of the planet grows, so does the demand for oil. But as cars and factories burn this fuel, and other fuels like coal, they release carbon dioxide into the atmosphere. Scientists now believe that this added carbon dioxide may slowly increase the temperature of the planet. They are using measurements taken on Earth, measurements taken by satellites, and sophisticated computer programs to understand the consequences for the Earth's climate.

 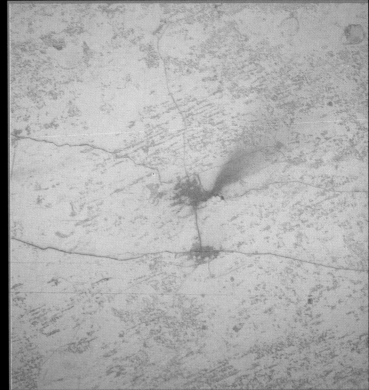

People have always poured their waste into the water and the air. When the human population was small, this pollution did not seriously affect the environment. The waters stayed clean because microscopic creatures were able to digest most of the waste. Winds of fresh air scattered the smoke from small fires.

Today there are so many people that many rivers are loaded with waste and many cities are covered in a smoggy haze. The Rhone River in France carries chemicals and sewage dumped into it by the factories, farms, and towns along its banks. Its cloudy, polluted water empties into the Mediterranean Sea (*above left*).

Even in small towns, like this one in the middle of Russia (*above right*), thick, black smoke billows out of factory smokestacks.

Over the few short years of the space age, astronauts have watched pollution like this increase all around the globe.

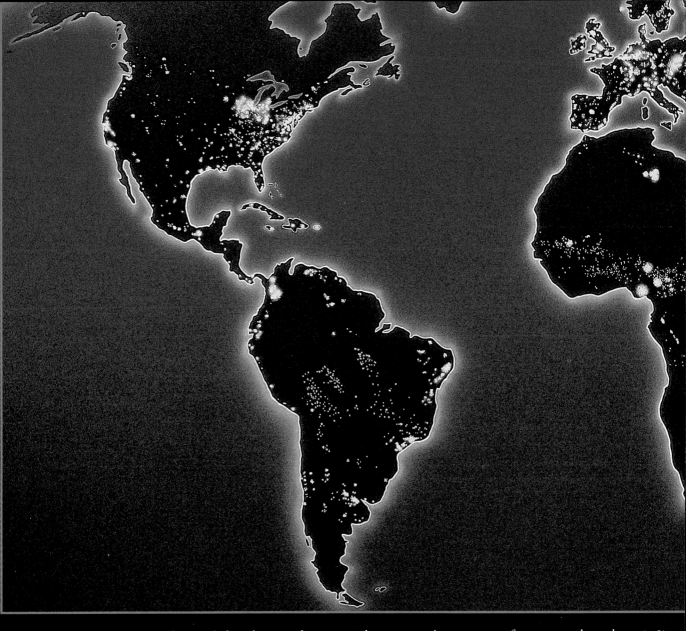

This view of the Earth at night shows that people are an important force on the planet. It was made from satellite data collected over many months, and it shows what each part of the Earth looks like on a cloudless night.

Some of the biosphere is almost uninhabited. The deserts are black and empty. Fires burn at oil fields in oil-rich countries around the Persian Gulf. Lights along the banks of the Nile River trace its path against the almost total darkness of the Sahara Desert.

The dark rain forests are dotted with lights from huge fires set to clear the land.

City lights outline every continent. Major cities like Los Angeles, Shanghai, and Madrid show up as bright balls of light. In some parts of the world—the eastern United States, Europe, and Japan—the lights of the cities blend together until it's difficult to tell where one stops and another starts.

Our planet is different from any other. As we explore the Earth, we are learning about its oceans, atmosphere, land, and life. We are finally beginning to understand our home planet and how we are affecting it.

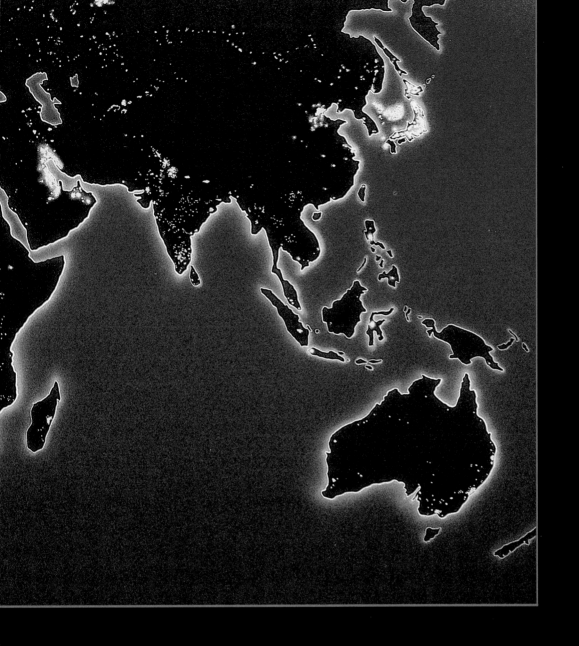

ABOUT THE AUTHORS

SALLY RIDE has been interested in science since she was a child. She earned bachelor's degrees in physics and English and a Ph.D. in physics at Stanford University. In 1983 she became America's first woman astronaut when she made a six-day flight aboard the Space Shuttle *Challenger*. She made her second Shuttle flight in 1984. Dr. Ride left NASA in 1987, and is now director of the California Space Institute at the University of California, San Diego, where she is a professor of physics.

TAM O'SHAUGHNESSY and Sally Ride have been friends since they were both competing in national junior tennis tournaments. Ms. O'Shaughnessy went on to compete professionally before studying biology. She holds master's degrees in biology and education, and is studying learning disabilities at the University of California, Riverside, for her Ph.D. Ms. O'Shaughnessy lives in La Jolla, California, where she teaches biology and counsels students at San Diego Mesa College.

INDEX